*For my son, Tim, who is deciding
what to do with the rest of his life.*

First published in hardback in Great Britain by Andersen Press Ltd in 1998
First published in paperback by Picture Lions in 2000
This edition published by Collins Picture Books in 2002

1 3 5 7 9 10 8 6 4 2
ISBN: 0-00-714012-6

Picture Lions and Collins Picture Books are imprints of the Children's Division, part of HarperCollins Publishers Ltd.
Text and illustrations copyright © Colin McNaughton 1998
The author/illustrator asserts the moral right to be identified as the author/illustrator of the work.
A CIP catalogue record for this title is available from the British Library.
All rights reserved. No part of this publication may be reproduced, stored in a retrieval system or transmitted in any
form or by any means, electronic, mechanical, photocopying, recording or otherwise, without the prior permission
of HarperCollins Publishers Ltd, 77-85 Fulham Palace Road, Hammersmith, London W6 8JB.

The HarperCollins website address is: www.fireandwater.com

Printed in Hong Kong

No animals were hurt in the
making of this book. Oh, except
Mister Wolf, of course.

Colin McNaughton

Hmm...

Collins

An imprint of HarperCollinsPublishers

One fine day…

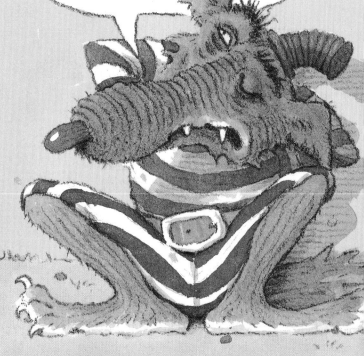

"Well, clever chops," said Mister Wolf. "What sort of job do you suggest?"

"Well," said Preston, "what do you want to be?"

"Hmm…" said Mister Wolf. "Full-up."

"What are you good at?" said Preston.

"Hmm…" said Mister Wolf.
"Eating pigs."

"And what do you enjoy?"
said Preston.

"Hmm…" said Mister Wolf.
"Eating pigs *and* being full-up."

"You could be a footballer," said Preston.

"Hmm…" said Mister Wolf. "I wouldn't mind a shot at that."

"You could be an astronaut," said Preston.

"Hmm…" said Mister Wolf. "I'd be over the moon with that."

"You could be a school teacher," said Preston.

"Hmm…" said Mister Wolf. "I could certainly teach you a lesson or two!"

"You could be a pilot," said Preston.

"Hmm…" said Mister Wolf. "That would suit me down to the ground."

"You could be a poet," said Preston.

"Hmm…" said Mister Wolf. "I could do verse, I suppose."

"You could be a crane driver," said Preston.

"Hmm…" said Mister Wolf. "That's a smashing idea!"

"You could be a sailor," said Preston.

"Hmm…" said Mister Wolf. "I could take that idea on board."

"You could be a cook,"
said Preston.

"Hmm…" said Mister Wolf.
"A very tasty idea!"

"So, Mister Wolf,"
said Preston,
"what do you think?"

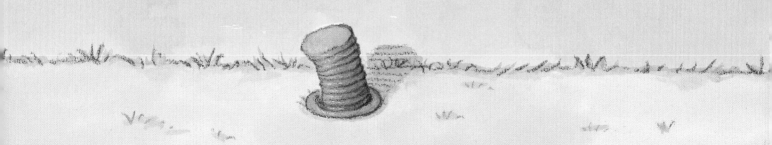

"Hmm…" said Mister Wolf.
"It's certainly food
for thought!"

Suddenly!

Collect all the Preston Pig Stories

Colin McNaughton
Suddenly!
Look behind you, Preston Pig!

0-00-714013-4

Colin McNaughton
GOAL!
Go football crazy with Preston Pig!

0-00-714011-8

Colin McNaughton
BOO!
Surprise! It's Preston Pig!

0-00-714014-2

Colin McNaughton
Oops!
I'm coming to get you, Preston Pig!

0-00-714015-0

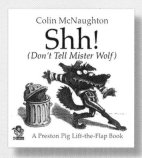
Colin McNaughton
Shh!
(Don't Tell Mister Wolf)
A Preston Pig Lift-the-Flap Book

0-00-664715-4

Colin McNaughton
Hmm...
Who's hungry for Preston Pig?

0-00-714012-6

Colin McNaughton
Oomph!
Fall in love with Preston Pig!

0-00-712635-2

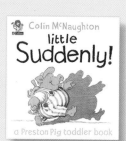
Colin McNaughton
little
Suddenly!
a Preston Pig toddler book

0-00-713235-2

Colin McNaughton
little
Oops!
a Preston Pig toddler book

0-00-713236-0

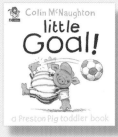
Colin McNaughton
little
Goal!
a Preston Pig toddler book

0-00-713234-4

Colin McNaughton
little
Boo!
a Preston Pig toddler boo[k]

0-00-713237-9

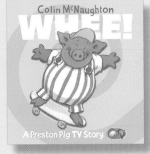
Colin McNaughton
WHEE!
A Preston Pig TV Story CiTV

0-00-712371-X

Colin McNaughton
POOH!
A Preston Pig TV Story CiTV

0-00-712370-1

Colin McNaughton
PARP!
A Preston Pig TV Story CiTV

0-00-712372-8

Colin McNaughton is one of Britain's most highly-acclaimed picture book talents and a winner of many prestigious awards. His Preston Pig Stories are hugely successful with Preston now starring in his own animated television series on CITV.